The Billy Goats Gruff

Retold by Jane Bingham

Illustrated by
Daniel Postgate

Reading Consultant: Alison Kelly
University of Surrey Roehampton

Contents

Chapter 1

On the farm

We're the Gruff brothers.

Once upon a time, three billy goats lived on a farm, in the shadow of a mountain. They were brothers and their last name was Gruff.

Beanie was the youngest. He was small and skinny, always hungry...

and always in trouble.

Bertie was the middle
brother.

He was crazy about sports.

Biffer was the oldest. He was big and strong and looked after his brothers.

Chapter 2

Time to go

One winter, there was very little food on the farm.

"I'm so hungry," moaned Beanie, "I've only eaten a piece of hay today."

"Fibber," said Bertie, "I saw you at the clothesline earlier. You ate two socks and a shirt."

Biffer was worried. "I think it's time we made a move," he said. "We'll starve if we stay here."

"Where will we go?" asked Beanie.

"To the Juicy Fields beyond the hills," Biffer replied. "No one lives there, so we'll have plenty of food. We just have to cross the Rushing River."

Bertie looked terrified. "We can't go over the river!" he cried. "That's where the Terrible Troll lives."

"He's huge and green," said Beanie. "He'll gobble us up."

"Don't be silly," Biffer said. "There's no such thing as trolls. That's farmyard talk."

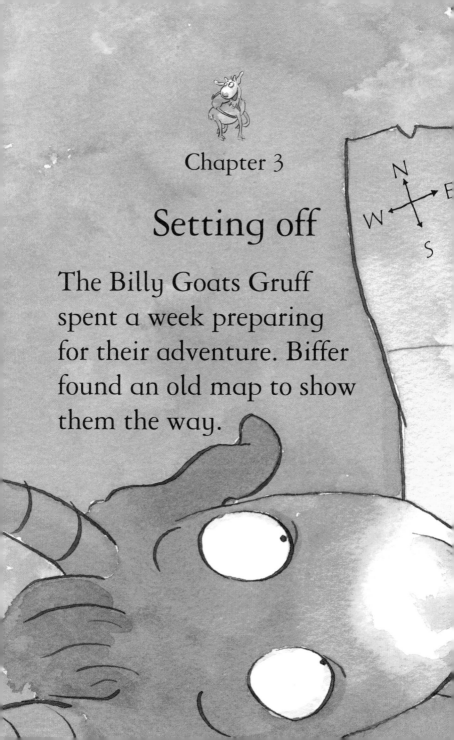

Chapter 3

Setting off

The Billy Goats Gruff
spent a week preparing
for their adventure. Biffer
found an old map to show
them the way.

Then Beanie and Bertie
had to learn to climb
up hills.

Oof!

Beanie was better
at coming down.

After a few days, they were both excellent climbers.

Finally, the brothers had to pack for their journey.

At last, the Billy Goats Gruff were ready to set off. All the other farm animals came to say goodbye.

16

The younger animals wanted to go too. But the older ones shook their heads. "Let's hope they make it past the bridge," they muttered.

17

Chapter 4

Into the forest

Bertie and Beanie were still dreaming of the Juicy Fields as they left the farm.

18

Ahead of them loomed the Dark Forest.

"I'm not sure I want to go in there," said Beanie.

"We'll be fine," said Biffer, "as long as we stick together."

What's that thudding noise?

It's Bertie's ball.

The billy goats trotted along the path. The only sound was the tap-tap-tapping of their hooves on the forest floor.

Suddenly, a thick mist swirled around them.

I can hardly see my feet.

Beanie shivered. "I don't like this forest. It's spooky," he said. "Do you think there might be ghosts here?"

"Yes," said Bertie, with a grin. "Lots of ghosts. And more than anything, ghosts like scaring little billy goats."

"Shut up, Bertie," said Biffer sternly. "Stop scaring Beanie."

The billy goats walked on in silence.

"Um, Biffer?" Beanie said after a while.

"Yes, Beanie?"

"I think someone's following us."

Listen!

The billy goats stopped and listened. They strained their ears... and heard a thumping sound. It grew louder with every second.

"Oh no," shrieked Beanie. "Look behind us!" A strange shape was coming down the path – and it was heading straight for them.

It's a ghost!

"Run!" cried Bertie. "Run for your lives."

Before Biffer could stop
them, Beanie and Bertie had
raced off down the path.

We've got to
stick together!

"Come back," Biffer shouted.
"It's not a ghost. It's a..."

Biffer waited, as the shape slowly appeared out of the mist. "It's only a rabbit," he said.

Don't be so rude!

"I'm not *only* a rabbit," said the rabbit. "I'm a rare breed of tall, lop-eared rabbit and my name is Buffy."

"I'm Biffer. Nice to meet you," said Biffer quickly, "but I must find my brothers before they get lost."

Sorry, no time to chat.

"Where are you going?" Buffy asked.

"To the Juicy Fields by the mountains," Biffer called, running after his brothers.

"Watch out for the troll," Buffy shouted after him. Biffer didn't hear. He had already headed deeper into the forest.

Oh dear. No one's ever made it past the troll.

Chapter 5

Tricking the troll

Hello? Anyone there?

Meanwhile, Bertie was wandering alone through the forest. He had lost Beanie in the mist and he didn't know which way to go.

Beanie had been luckier. He had found the path that ran straight through the forest.

Whew! That was close.

"I can't wait to get to the Juicy Fields," Beanie thought, as he headed to the river.

The only way to cross the Rushing River was over a little wooden bridge. Next to the bridge was a big wooden sign.

WARNING

Goats

beware!

"I wish I could read," thought Beanie.

His hooves went clippety-clop, clippety-clop over the bridge. But as he reached the middle of the river...

...a large, green hand smashed through the wooden planks and grabbed Beanie's leg.

Beanie screamed.

"Who's that going over my bridge?" roared a terrible voice. "I'm coming to gobble you up!"

Beanie's eyes bulged with terror. There, crouched under the bridge, was a fat and warty troll.

"Please don't eat me," cried Beanie. "I'm only a little goat. My big brother is coming behind me. He'll be much tastier than me."

I'm sure you'd rather eat him.

"I think I can wait a little longer for my dinner," said the troll. "Now get off my bridge."

Shaking with fear, Beanie wobbled off the bridge and went to hide in some bushes. "I hope Bertie can save himself," he thought.

Chapter 6

Bertie on the bridge

Bertie arrived soon after and trotted onto the bridge – clappety-clop-bonk, clappety-clop-bonk. (He was bouncing his ball.)

"Who's that bouncing over my bridge?" bellowed the troll.

Oh no!

Bertie peered over the bridge, and gulped. "I didn't think trolls were real," he said.

"I'm real and I'm hungry,"
said the troll, "and I'm coming
to gobble you up!"

"You'll make a
very tasty meal,"
the troll went on.
"Nice fresh billy
goat. Yum, yum."

"Stop!" cried Bertie,
thinking quickly. "You can't
eat me. I'm only a medium-
sized billy goat. My big
brother is coming behind
me. He's much fatter."

What big teeth
he has...

"Humph," said the troll, rubbing his stomach. "I'll wait for the fattest one then. He had better be juicy."

Chapter 7

Brave Biffer

At last, Biffer came out of the forest. When he spotted his brothers on the other side of the river, he raced to the bank.

40

Beanie and Bertie leaped
out of the bushes, waving their
hooves wildly.

"Stop Biffer!" they cried.
"STOP! There's a troll under
the bridge."

It was too late. Biffer was already crossing. His heavy hooves went clunkety-clop, clunkety-clop and the bridge strained under his weight.

By this time, the troll was starving.

"Who's that stomping over my bridge?" he roared.

I'm going to gobble you up!

But Biffer stood his ground. "I'm an enormous billy goat," Biffer said, "and I'm ready for a fight."

Biffer lowered his head and caught the troll on his horns.

He bounced the troll into the air. Then, with a toss of his head, Biffer whacked him into the Rushing River.

The troll landed with an
enormous SPLASH. He sank
under the water and was never
seen again.

Beanie and Bertie couldn't believe it.

"You're the best, Biffer!" they cried.

Just then, a stream of animals came out of the forest – deer, squirrels, rabbits and foxes. In a large crowd, they skipped across the bridge.

"Where are you going?"
Biffer asked a rabbit.

"We're off to the Juicy
Fields," she replied. "We've
been trapped in the forest for
years, because of the troll.
Now, at last, we're free."

Our hero!

I hope there'll
be enough
food...

This retelling of *The Billy Goats Gruff* is based on the folktale from Norway.

Edited by Susanna Davidson

Designed by Russell Punter
and Natacha Goransky

Series editor: Lesley Sims

First published in 2004 by Usborne Publishing Ltd., Usborne House,
83-85 Saffron Hill, London EC1N 8RT, England. www.usborne.com
Copyright © 2004 Usborne Publishing Ltd.